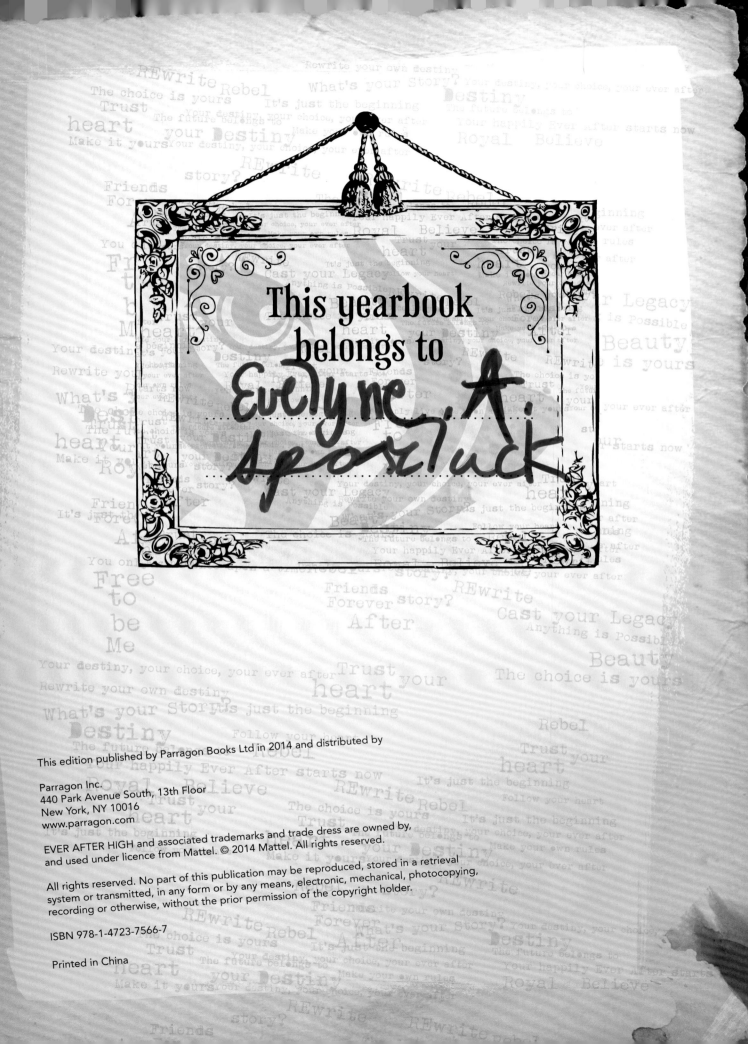

This yearbook belongs to

Evelyne A. Spoxluck

This edition published by Parragon Books Ltd in 2014 and distributed by

Parragon Inc.
440 Park Avenue South, 13th Floor
New York, NY 10016
www.parragon.com

EVER AFTER HIGH and associated trademarks and trade dress are owned by, and used under licence from Mattel. © 2014 Mattel. All rights reserved.

ISBN 978-1-4723-7566-7

Printed in China

Ever After High™

Royals and Rebels

PaRragon

Bath • New York • Cologne • Melbourne • Delhi
Hong Kong • Shenzhen • Singapore • Amsterdam

❧ Contents ❧

Welcome to Ever After High

Welcome, dear student. Come hither and let me look upon you. Be not afraid to enter the presence of Baba Yaga. Ah! I see that you are young, and like all students at Ever After High, your story is just beginning. You have many hexciting lessons to learn as you travel through life, but this school will point you on the path to understanding the complex and vital relationship between prewritten destiny and free will.

I am sure we will meet often during your time here. As well as my role as Faculty Advisor, I teach classes in spells, hexes, and general witchery and am often called upon to spiritually guide and mentor individual students. For now, however, on behalf of our esteemed headmaster, Milton Grimm, and the entire staff, may I wish you a hexcellent first term at Ever After High.

Baba Yaga

A Royally Rebellious Tale

Are you sitting comfortably? Then I'll begin.

Once upon a time . . .

here was a boarding school called Ever After High. The students of this school were the children of fairy-tale legends, and their education involved learning to embrace and relive their parents' destinies.

One fine Legacy Day, the new students lined up to sign the *Storybook of Legends*—the magical book that binds students to their destinies. Apple White, daughter of Snow White, stepped forward, her flowing locks glimmering in the sunlight. With a flick and a flourish of her quill, Apple White bonded herself to her predestined future.

Apple, like all students at Ever After High, was certain that failure to sign the *Storybook of Legends* would spell The End. According to Ever After High's headmaster, Milton Grimm, refusal to sign meant your story would fade into oblivion. You would cease to exist, taking with you all those whose destinies were entwined with your own.

Next, 'twas the turn of Raven Queen, daughter of the infamous Evil Queen. Raven knew that legend had cast her as the villain, poisoning apples and causing chaos, misery, and mayhem. So, although she knew she was key to others' Happily Ever Afters, this was not a future she wanted to accept.

Stepping away from the book and casting down her quill, Raven refused to sign the book and rejected her destiny . . . preferring to create her own.

With that one gesture, all was altered. Questions floated into the air. Why hadn't Raven Queen and Apple White vanished? Was it possible that a person could be free to write their own story and create their own destiny?

Life at Ever After High changed forever. Students with royal connections and a promised Happily Ever After believed that accepting who you are and the path you have inherited is the key to happiness. The more rebellious and free-thinking students like Raven, whose original legends were less enticing, now allowed themselves to hope that they can find true joy by forging their own future.

And so it was that the student body became split into two factions— the Royals and the Rebels. So different, yet so alike. Divided by their approach to destiny, yet united in their quest to find a Happily Ever After.

Meet the Roomies

Apple White

My Story so Far . . . .

"Mirror, Mirror, on the wall, who is the fairest in the school halls"

Well hello! I'm Apple White, daughter of Snow White. I may not have inherited my mother's ebony-colored hair, but I do have her knack for bringing cute animals to my side whenever I sing. Also, like her, I royally lose control whenever I see a yummy apple! I believe in working hard to follow your destiny. Isn't that enchanting? I just know my Happily Ever After is right around the corner.

Roommate
Raven Queen. I'm rooming with Raven rather than Briar Beauty this year—after all, our destinies are forever entwined!

Best Friends Forever After
Briar Beauty and Blondie Lockes.

Storybook Romance Status
Sure I find Prince Daring Charming, well . . . charming. We're destined for each other, but we're definitely not an item—yet!

Heart's Desire
I hope that one day everyone in the kingdom will understand that my beauty is not just skin deep. I try to be fair inside and out.

Favorite Subject
I always hocus focus in Kingdom Management Class. I take my role as future queen very seriously.

Worst Subject
Cooking Class-ic. I swear someone keeps trying to slip poison into my food.

Raven Queen

My Story so Far . . . .

OK, so I'm the daughter of the dark sorceress, the Evil Queen, and yes, like my mother I can cast terrible spells—but forget what you think you know about me. Ever since I refused to sign the *Storybook of Legends* on Legacy Day, everyone at this school has an opinion about me, especially Apple White. The thing is, I'm not interested in following in anyone's footsteps. I'm my own person and, although I can't change what others think of me, I can change my destiny.

> "Don't judge a book by its cover!"

Roommate
Apple White. I can't believe I'm sharing a dorm with someone who's so up in my story! When is she going to get the message that I'm just never going to poison her?

Best Friends Forever After
Madeline Hatter and Cerise Hood.

Storybook Romance Status
Single and staying that way. I need to figure out where I'm going before I take someone else along for the ride.

Heart's Desire
To be allowed to stay true to myself.

Favorite Subject
Muse-ic Class. I may not be evil, but I've got a wicked voice!

Worst Subject
Magicology. Enough with the spells already.

Meet the Roomies

Briar Beauty

My Story so Far . . . .

Enchanted to make your acquaintance! I'm Briar Beauty—but you probably know that, unless you've been asleep for a hundred years! My own destiny includes a lengthy nap, but it'll be worth it just to be kissed awake by a handsome hunk. Just imagine how fairy fresh and fabulous I'll look after all that beauty sleep! In the meantime, I'll be busy planning the next Ever After High get-together.

"Life's a dream!"

Roommate

Ashlynn Ella. Ashlynn's great, but I just sometimes wish she'd channel her inner Rapunzel, you know—loosen up and let her hair down!

Best Friends Forever After

Apple White and Blondie Lockes.

Storybook Romance Status

I'm waiting to lock eyes with my perfect prince across a crowded dance floor.

Heart's Desire

To live life to the fairy-tale fullest. You never know when you're going to prick your finger and slip into a century-long coma.

Favorite Subject

It's really more an activity. My role on the Royal Student Council (from Throncoming to Prom) is a party planner's dream!

Worst Subject

Grimmnastics. Swap my gorgeous gown for sweaty shorts? No thanks!

Ashlynn Ella™

My Story so Far....

I'm the daughter of Cinderella. Just like my mother, I know that fate is going to take me on a rollercoaster ride! I'm destined to lose my wealth and get stuck with a nightmare stepfamily before I can meet my prince. Surprisingly, I'm totally OK with that, even if it means a heap of housework and killer blisters—glass shoes really chafe!—just as long as I'm actually in love. If I happen to fall for a handsome outdoorsman instead, it'll be a different fairy tale entirely!

"Let's not start off on the wrong slipper!"

Roommate
Briar Beauty. We both may be Royal, but we don't always see eye-to-eye.

Best Friends Forever After
Apple White and Raven Queen.

Storybook Romance Status
Shhh! You can't breathe a word . . . I'm dating Hunter Huntsman. We're from different worlds, but we're made for each other.

Heart's Desire
To marry for true love—it's the only way to a Happily Ever After.

Favorite Subject
Environmental Magic. It's important I set an example for others by caring for our world.

Worst Subject
Princessology 101. Sit up straight, curtsey to the prince on your right before the prince on your left . . . blah, blah, blah—yawn!

Meet the Roomies

Madeline Hatter™

My Story so Far . . . .

White knight, sunshine: a place, a face, I have mine? Oh, sorry, you probably don't speak Riddlish! I was just asking your name. I'm Madeline, but you can call me Maddie. I come from Wonderland, where Riddlish is uncommonly spoken, so I can understand almost everything Giles Grimm says. He's the headmaster's brother, but Mr. Grimm put a Babble Spell on him, and now he lives in the Vault of Lost Tales. Oops, see, I'm rambling again!

"Ever After High is just Hat-tastic!"

Roommate

Kitty Cheshire. I have the strangest feeling that we're two of a kind, if only she didn't keep vanishing!

Best Friends Forever After

Kitty Chesire and Lizzie Hearts—they are the only ones who understand each other.

Storybook Romance Status

I'd love to fall crazy-in-love. I'm just looking for someone to match my crazy streak!

Heart's Desire

To run the greatest Hat & Tea Shoppe the world has ever known!

Favorite Subject

Chemythstry. I love mixing growing and shrinking potions.

Worst Subject

Debate. I tend to yabber on and when I get into Riddlish . . . well, I'm pretty hard to understand.

Kitty Cheshire™

My Story so Far....

"Poof!" Ah, here I am, and here you are. I may stay a while, but then again, I may not—it depends on whether you can keep my attention. So, you want to know all about me and possibly about Carrolloo, my Wonderland caterpillar friend? Well I won't tell you. Or will I? Who knows! If you need me, you could try my dorm, or just follow my yarn—I love to knit. It might lead you to me . . . but then again, it may not. So long! "Poof!"

"Don't worry, just smile!"

Roommate
Madeline Hatter. She really rubs me up the wrong way.

Best Friends Forever After
I prefer Wonderlanders.

Storybook Romance Status
I haven't met my pawfect tomcat yet!

Heart's Desire
To be misunderstood. I unravel order like a ball of yarn at every turn.

Favourite Subject
Geografairy. I like to know the lay of the land, so I can appear anywhere suddenly.

Worst Subject
Swim Class. Cats and water? Say no more!

Meet the Roomies

Cerise Hood

My Story so Far . . . .

Ggggrrr! I mean, hi, I didn't see you there. I'm Cerise Hood, daughter of Red Riding Hood. I'm just a regular student here at Ever After High; nothing strange about me.

I just happen to like running around the forest—with wolves. What am I hiding under my hood? Oh, err, that's just a family thing. I mean, cloaks are practical, right? And it's a statement look. Anyway, I have to go . . . .

"I'm cloaked in mystery."

Roommate
Cedar Wood. She's sweet and funny—but she sure likes to talk.

Best Friends Forever After
Raven Queen, Maddie Hatter, and Cedar Wood.

Storybook Romance Status
Single. One day I'd like to find a pack leader who loves me—ears, claws, and all.

Heart's Desire
To be open about my Big Bad Secret.

Favorite Subject
Cross Country Running—there's no one faster at EAH.

Worst Subject
Any class where we have to work on group projects. I'm kind of a loner.

Cedar Wood™

My Story so Far . . . .

Hello, I'm Cedar, daughter of Pinocchio. I don't want to be doing this right now. There's somewhere else I'd rather be. Sorry, the truth can be hurtful; but I just cannot tell a lie! I share my father's destiny. I'm a wooden puppet learning how to become a real child. Being wooden sounds tough, but it's not all bad—I don't feel pain and I'm a wicked swimmer!

"Honest to goodness!"

Roommate
Cerise Hood. She was a hard nut to crack, but we're firm friends now.

Best Friends Forever After
Raven Queen, Cerise Hood, and Maddie Hatter.

Storybook Romance Status
One day I'm sure I'll find a real boyfriend to date.

Heart's Desire
To become flesh and blood and be able to make my own choices, just like a real girl.

Favorite Subject
Arts and Crafts. Painting and drawing are the only times I can exaggerate!

Worst Subject
Woodwork. Sawing, sanding . . . it's like a horror film in that class!

Meet the Roomies

Blondie Lockes™

My Story so Far . . . .

Knock knock! It's Blondie! Actually, I never need to knock—I can pick any lock and walk right in. And why wouldn't I? I'm curious by nature and sweet as sugar-laden porridge, so people are always pleased to see me. Well, mostly pleased, anyway. I know chapter and verse about the comings and thronings at this school—my MirrorCast show gets a cauldron load of viewers!

> "Just right, never wrong."

Roommate
C.A. Cupid. My MirrorCast show is one of the hottest so I can open many doors for her!

Best Friends Forever After
Apple White and Briar Beauty.

Storybook Romance Status
I'm currently single, but I just know my perfect prince is out there somewhere.

Heart's Desire
To find a royal destiny that's "just right" for me.

Favorite Subject
Debate. Hear ye! Hear ye! Or should that be "Hear me! Hear me!"? I have very strong opinions on countless subjects.

Worst Subject
Arts and Crafts—why would anyone critique my work?

C.A. Cupid ™

My Story so Far....

Hi girls! I broadcast my own radio show from catacombs—until my dad, Eros, decided that my destiny lies at Ever After High. Things are changing for the students here, and they need a guide to help them discover their hearts' desires. So, my *Love Matters* advice show on the MirrorCast network is really popular. But what about my secret heart's desire? Now that I've arrived at a new school I feel more confused than ever!

> "I'm all about the 'Happily Ever After!'"

Roommate
Blondie Lockes. We are both part of the school MirrorCast.

Best Friends Forever After
Royals, rebels, and anyone with love in their heart.

Storybook Romance Status
It's not a romance . . . yet. I've set my bow and arrows for Prince Dexter Charming; but he likes Raven, so we're just friends.

Heart's Desire
To help everyone find true love—including myself.

Favorite Subject
Ancient History. Eros adopted me, so I want to learn everything I can about my heritage and place in the world.

Worst Subject
Crownculus. Not everything can be solved with an equation.

Meet the Roomies

Dexter Charming

Good day. Oh, no, I'm not Daring. I'm not sure where you'll find my brother—probably in the castleteria. Anyway, enchanted to make your acquaintance. I hope we meet again!

Roommate

Hunter Huntsman. I mainly just try to stay on the opposite side of the room from his axe!

Best Friends Forever After

My brother Daring.

Storybook Romance Status

Err, I, err, um, I, you see, err . . . it's, err, Raven, err. Oh curses! I wish I could just tell her how I feel.

Heart's Desire

It's like my friend C.A. Cupid says—I must follow my heart and find true love, with whomever loves me truly.

Favorite Subject

Hero Training. I want to be the best that I can be.

Worst Subject

Wooing 101—even the thought of this class brings me out in a cold sweat.

"I'd love to be a hextbook prince!"

Hunter Huntsman™

Hello there. Hunter Huntsman at your service. How may I be of assistance? If you wish to learn more about me, be my guest!

Roommate

Dexter Charming—he's pretty quiet, but he seems like a good kid.

Best Friends Forever After

Daring, Dexter, and Ashlynn.

Storybook Romance Status

Ashlynn Ella and I are kindred spirits. I hope we won't always have to hide our love for each other.

Heart's Desire

To be a force for good.

Favorite Subject

Beast Training and Care. I love animals.

Worst Subject

Diplomacy 101. Castles and kingly pursuits make me claustrophobic. I'm an outdoorsman.

"Truth, justice, and the woodland way!"

Daring Charming

Good morrow, fair maiden. Are you in distress? I have to see a knave about a dragon, but I'll be back. Never fear.

Roommate
Hopper Croakington II. He's a good guy, even if he sometimes turns into a toad.

Best Friends Forever After
My bro Dexter and Hopper Croakington.

Storybook Romance Status
Yeah, Apple is sweet and we're destined to be an item, but why should the other ladies at school miss out on a slice of charming?

Heart's Desire
To live the single life to the max while I can—and to be given a true heroic deed to do.

Favorite Subject
Theater. I was born to take center stage!

Worst Subject
Dragon Slaying. I rock at it, but it's so simple it bores me.

"Charmed, I'm sure!"

Hopper Croakington II

Hopper Croakington II is my full title. You want to talk to me? I'm flattered, you're so . . . RIBBIT!

Roommate
Daring Charming—the Prince, the legend!

Best Friends Forever After
Daring, Dexter, and any available princesses.

Storybook Romance Status
Anyone I can woo with poetry, but there is someone special. Oh what prize could be much higher, than a date with beauty Briar?

Heart's Desire
To be loved by someone—warts and all.

Favorite Subject
Advanced Wooing—one never stops learning (and crashing in flames).

Worst Subject
Kingdom Management. Bah! There's plenty of time for that when I'm king.

"To woo or not to woo, that is the question!"

Briar's Beauty-ful Dream

Royal napper Briar Beauty has drifted off in the middle of her Home Economyths Class! What is happening in the princess's dream? Use your sense of wonder and fairy-tale imagination to draw the pictures in her mind's eye.

The Perfect party

Use paint,
pastels, or pens
to color your
art. Make it
magical!

Great Hexpectations

This year Raven has signed up to take a class in Advanced Allusions and Cross-Cultural References. Her first assignment is to discuss the idea of "destiny". What do you think your future holds?

Time to Hocus Focus!

Use this parchment to write a story . . . starring you. What will happen? What friends will share your adventure? What sort of person will you become? Who knows, your ideas might even sow the seeds of your own perfect Happily Ever After!

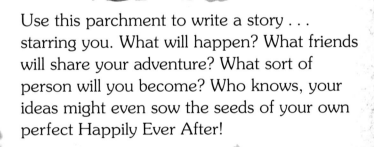

Wooing 101

All princes need to perfect their wooing techniques—that's why they attend Wooing 101 class at EAH. Take this simple test to discover which handsome hunk or perfect prince would win you over. Just answer "Hex Yeah" or "Fairy Fail" to each question, then follow the arrows across the page.

Did it hurt . . . when you fell from heaven?

Shall we take a walk in the enchanted forest?

FAIRY FAIL

HEX YEAH

Do you believe in love at first sight? Or should I walk by again?

FAIRY FAIL

FAIRY FAIL

HEX YEAH

FAIRY FAIL

HEX YEAH

Daring Charming
Son of King Charming

You'll be hex-tatic to discover that Daring's your guy! He's gorgeous, confident, and outgoing. Oh, just get ready to share your magic mirror.

Hopper Croakington II
Son of the Frog Prince

You love a romantic, and Hopper is certainly that— even if his courting technique is a toad on the sleazy side.

Hunter Huntsman
Son of the Huntsman

Handsome, hunky Hunter is axe-olutely perfect for you. Honest, brave, and kind, he'll always have your back.

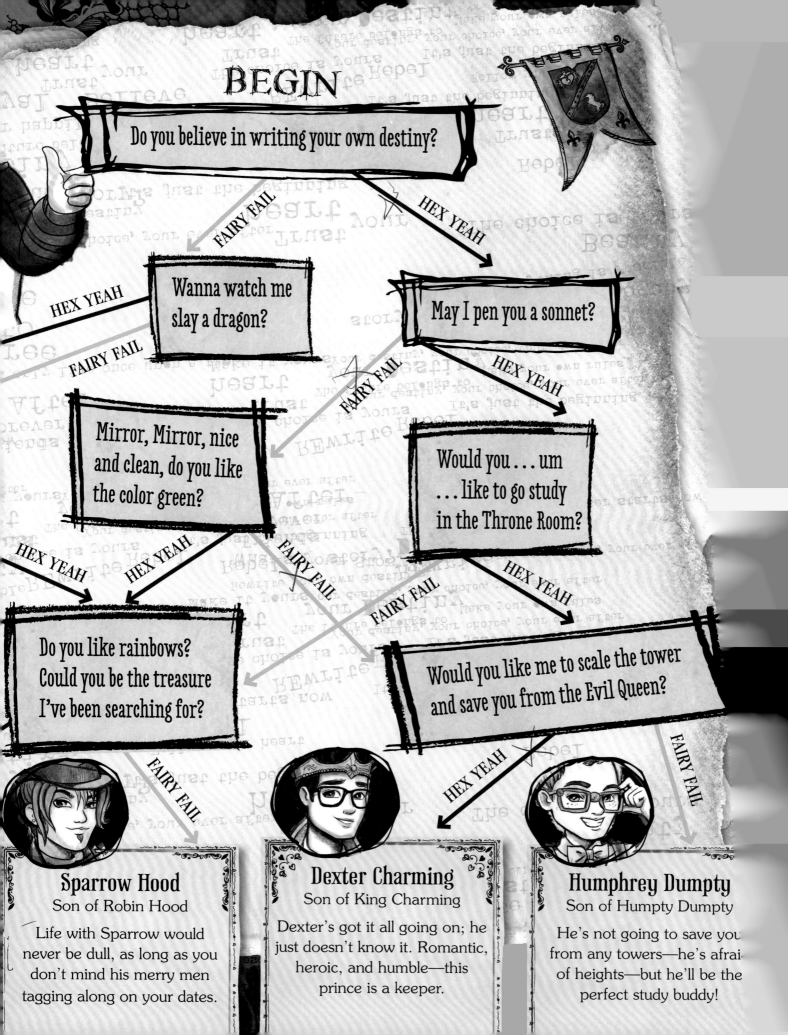

Quiz for a Queen

Holly O'Hair's destiny may see her crowned one day! As the daughter of Rapunzel, Holly believes that a queen should be as intelligent as she is beautiful. Having been home-schooled in the tower for so long, Holly's eager to throw herself into school life. Today she's busy studying the truth behind the legends for Princessology class. Hold her hair (I mean, hand) and take the test with her.

1 In Snow White's legend, she was so named because . . .

a) of her bright blonde hair

b) of her white skin

c) she was born on the day it began to snow.

2 Briar Beauty, like her mother, is cursed to . . .

a) fall asleep for 100 years

b) fall asleep for 1,000 years

c) fall asleep and never wake up.

3 What do these three students have in common?

Lizzie Hearts
Kitty Cheshire
Madeline Hatter

They are from Wonderland

4 What is strange about Madeline's hat?

You can pull anything out of it

5 Which girl at Ever After High is the inheritor of a legend featuring glass slippers and stepsisters?

Ashlyn Ella

6 Which mysterious girl at Ever After High has parents who have broken from their prewritten ~~fairy tale~~? What did they do?

~~Cedar wood~~

Cires hood. They got married

7 As well as from giving Snow White a poisoned apple, the Evil Queen had tried to kill her twice before. Which of these other attempts, according to legend, did not occur?

a) The Evil Queen laced Snow White's corset too tight, so that she couldn't breathe.

b) The Evil Queen dipped a comb in poison and gave it to Snow White to put in her hair.

c) The Evil Queen sent Snow White out to look for the dwarves in the dark, leading her to fall down a mineshaft.

8 Cedar Wood is to inherit the destiny of her father. Who is he?

Ponchiorw

9 Who at Ever After High could be seen as an unwelcome visitor with a liking for breakfast foods?

a) Cerise Hood

b) Holly O'Hair

c) Blondie Lockes ✓

10 Which Ever After High student is new in school? Which school did she transfer from?

C.A. Cupid

11 Which strange language is spoken in Wonderland?

Riddlish

12 The heir to the original legend of Robin Hood is called . . .

a) Hawk Hood

b) Sparrow Hood ✓

c) Eagle Hood

13 King Charming has two children at Ever After High. Name them.

Daring Charming and Dexter Charming

14 Name two legends with which Hunter Huntsman's destiny is heroically entwined.

little red riding hood and Snow White

15 Which original legend is part of Hopper Croakington II's heritage?

The Princess and the Frog.

Sports Day

It's Sports Day at Ever After High! It's the perfect occasion to get a taste of the heroism in some of the princes and the athleticism of girls like Cerise Hood. Try your dainty little hand at some of their sporting challenges!

Dragon Slaying

Read the game report for today's Dragon Slaying Contest, then fill in the results board.

Game Report

1. Daring won and wore red.
2. The boy wearing number 1 came in third.
3. Dexter beat the boy in yellow, but wasn't wearing number 2.
4. Only one boy finished in the same position as the number he wore, but he didn't wear red.
5. Sparrow beat the boy wearing number 3, and Hunter wore yellow. The boy in green wore number 2.
6. Cerise Hood, who was watching the contest, remembered that one boy wore blue.
7. She remembered that the final was between number 4 and number 2.

POSITION	NAME	NUMBER	COLOR
First Place	Daring		Red
Second Place	Hunter		Yellow
Third Place			
Fourth Place		B	

Basketball

This favorite game of Cerise Hood involves attempting to get the ball in the net, while carrying baskets of food for Grandma. Oh, and wolves chase you along the way! Hunter has dropped his basket. How many apples are scattered across the ground?

Wicked "Where?" Wordsearch

So, how are you settling in? Can you find your way around the school yet? Don't worry, it always takes a while. Fourteen Ever After High locations are hidden below. Can you find each one somewhere in the word square?

```
M I R O R L A M O O R C I E S U M A L S
O A G R I M M N A S I U M A E S T E R I
L O S E D F M I A N M I R G R E R E O M
C H D R M S T I R E S J C I G I A L U U
A A M O O R E N O R H T H L A R B S T S
H E S A D D G O B S O V I A N O I A T E
A N E T O N O C M U I R T B C T H E E L
L A N D L C E C H A R T L R R S O F C A
L I C D N E B K I C F M U A X I Q H M T
O O K E N D T H O F O F O Q B M A U I T
F T N A H C N E X O M F R D L R A C R S
A E C R O W D E R X B R I T M O N A R O
R D F I R Y T N O I K F R I H D O U D L
M R A N B Z O Z I O A O T M O O R R R F
O F A R G R F D L O S O E N C H A I L O
R O R L D R C H A R R A Y S L U L N E T
R R I L L A F O O I M U E U T R L O N L
R E U I B O K E U N D M U S E E U M F U
U A N C A S T M T E R O R N U I R R O A
C E N C H A N T E D F O R E S T R O F V
E C I F F O D E N W O R C D N A T S O L
```

BOOK END
CASTLETERIA
CAULDRON ROOM
CHARMITORIUM

DORMI-STORIES
ENCHANTED FOREST
GRIMMNASIUM
HALL OF ARMOR
LOST AND CROWNED OFFICE

MIRROR LAB
MUSE-EUM
MUSE-IC ROOM
THRONE ROOM
VAULT OF LOST TALES

Seekers can't give up! The words could be hiding in the most unhexpected corners of the square—they could even be printed backwards!

Apple's Fruity Feast

Apple White would give the keys to her kingdom to enjoy these tasty treats with Daring. Both dishes are full of scrumptious apples— her all-time favorite food!

Apple, Cheddar and Caramelized Onion Pizzettes

Ingredients for 4 pizzettes:

- 2 thinly sliced onions
- Olive or sunflower oil
- Handful of fresh thyme leaves
- 1 pack of small pre-made pizza bases
- 9oz pack of cheddar cheese, grated
- 2 apples, peeled, cored, and thinly sliced

Method:

1. Preheat the oven to 200°C/400°F/ Gas Mark 6.

2. Caramelize the onions by cooking them in a little oil over a medium heat until they are a rich-brown colour. Stir in the thyme and then take the pan off the heat.

3. Arrange the pizza bases on a baking sheet.

4. Divide the caramelized onion among the bases, spreading it evenly across each one.

5. Now sprinkle on a generous helping of cheddar, and then add the apple slices.

6. Bake the pizzettes in the oven, according to the base instructions. When they're ready, the cheese should be bubbly and the apple slices just turning golden brown.

Always check with an adult before using the kitchen—knives are sharp and ovens can be hot!

Ruby Red Apple Cupcakes

Ingredients for 12 cakes:

- 4oz self-rising flour
- 4oz superfine sugar
- 4oz butter
- 1 teaspoon of ground cinnamon
- 2 eggs
- 2 dessert apples, cored and chopped into small chunks
- 12 cupcake cases (preferably red or green)

Ingredients for the icing:

- 1 can of ready-made vanilla buttercream frosting
- 1 tube of red paste food coloring
- 1 pack of green ready-to-roll fondant icing
- Pretzel sticks or snapped pretzels

Method:

1. Preheat your oven to 190°C/375°F/Gas Mark 5.

2. Use a wooden spoon to mix together the flour, sugar, butter, and cinnamon. Make a well in the center of the mixture and break in the eggs.

3. Beat in the eggs until the mixture is smooth, then fold the chopped apple into the cake mixture.

4. Pour the mixture into the cake cases, dividing it equally.

5. Put the cakes into the oven. Bake them for around 15 minutes. When the cakes are golden and have domed tops, take them out and place them on a wire rack to cool.

6. Open the can of buttercream frosting and stir in a few drops of red food coloring.

7. Roll out the green icing. Carefully cut one or two leaf shapes for each cake.

8. Top each cake with a generous swirl of red icing—a knife or pallet knife is good for this. Stick a pretzel stick into the top of each one to make a stalk, then add a leaf or two. These look especially pretty when displayed in a basket on the table.

Witch Prof?

How well do you know the Ever After High faculty? Pore over each staff portrait, write the teacher's name below each frame, then add a line or two about what you might expect to do in a typical class. The list at the bottom of the page will help you.

A

Coach
Gingerbreadman

Grimmnastics

B

Professor Mamma
Bear

Home Economyths

C

Pro. Pappa Bear
Bear

Beast Training and Care

D

Mr. Jack B. Nimble

Environmental Magic

E

Pro. Rumpelstiltskin

Science and Sorcery,
Chemythstry

F

Professor Piper

Muse-ic

Professor Rumpelstiltskin
Mr. Jack B. Nimble

Professor Pied Piper
Coach Gingerbreadman

Professor Poppa Bear
Professor Momma Bear

Muse-ic Class

Hunter Huntsman and Ashlynn Ella don't go for public displays of affection. They're keeping their relationship under wraps. Hunter has decided to write a secret song with which to woo his girl. There's only one problem—Hunter's much happier wielding an axe than a pen. Can you help him pen a ballad befitting his beautiful princess?

SONG TITLE: "What's with Him?"

LYRICS: He's actin' crazy,
He's bein' weird,
He's been goin' crzy for me.
Oh, what's with him?
What's going on?

I think I know now.
He loves me!

Do You Speak Riddlish?

Maddie is visiting Giles Grimm in the Vault of Lost Tales. He has been cursed with the Babble Spell and talks in Riddlish. Luckily, Riddlish is spoken in Wonderland. Can you figure out these conversations? Match each Riddlish sentence to its translation on this page, and then write your own Riddlish on the facing page!

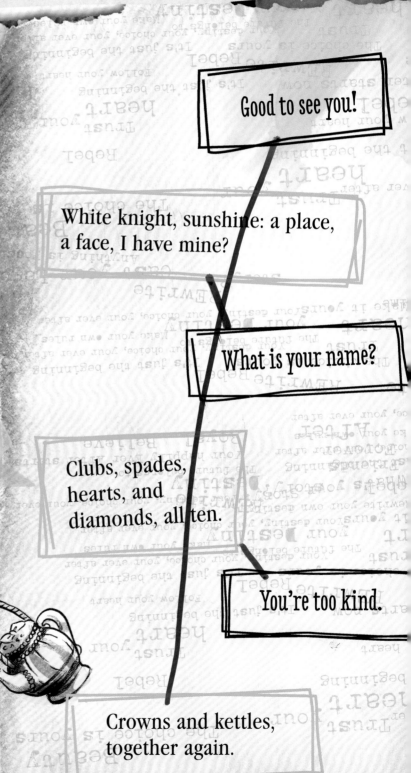

Good to see you!

White knight, sunshine: a place, a face, I have mine?

What is your name?

Clubs, spades, hearts, and diamonds, all ten.

You're too kind.

Crowns and kettles, together again.

How Riddlish Works

Riddlish is a unique language that uses rhymes and images to communicate ideas. There are no right or wrongs—every phrase is based on your own personal word associations.

1. Start by splitting a sentence into parts.
The sky / is blue.

2. Think of words or phrases associated with each part.
Above, clouds, flying / sadness, ocean, eyes.

3. Now combine them.
Above the clouds one often flies, not brown, but ocean-like the eyes.

Happy Riddlishing!

I like grass. / "7's a green

~~I like the color green.~~

I LIKE Grass / It is green

Love of green is the color

Castle *Design*

Both Daring and Dexter Charming love Castle Design class! In every class they get to plan and sketch their ultimate abode. Use this page to design your own future home. Will it be a cute cottage, a teetering tower(block), or a palatial pied-à-terre?

ONCE UPON A TIMES

The **school** newspaper needs a scoop. Create a front-page story based on one of the following school events. Don't forget to draw in pictures to illustrate your tale!

Legacy Day • True Hearts Day • Annual Dragon Slaying Contest

Look At Raven!

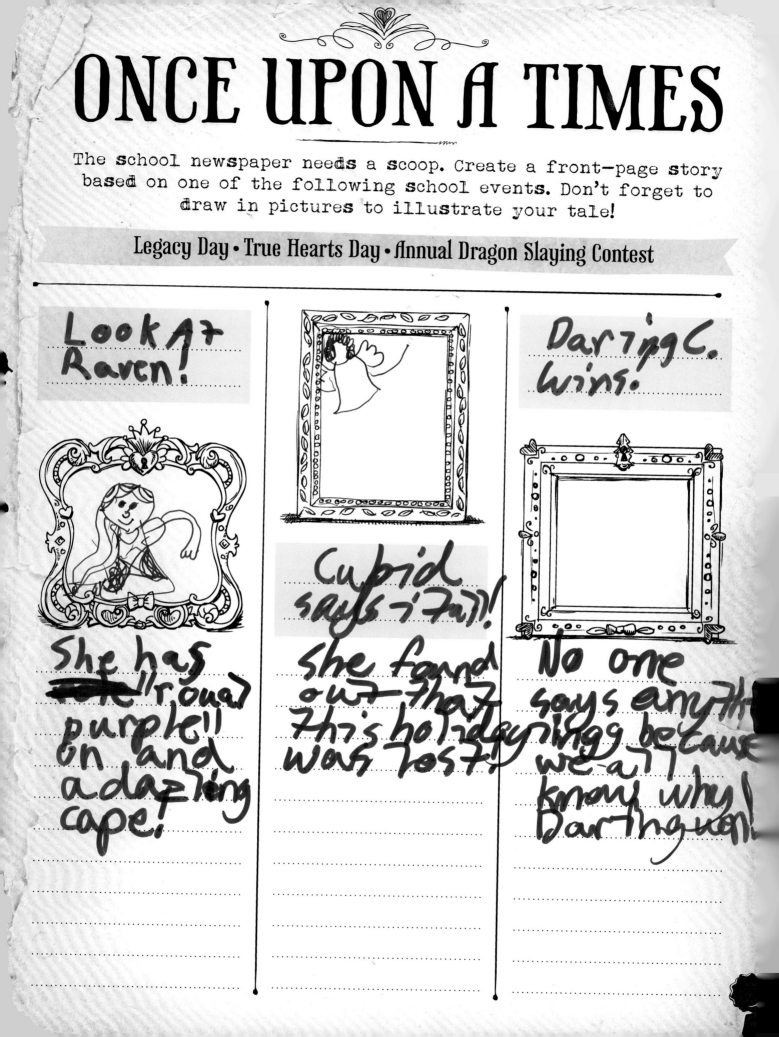

She has ~~the~~ ll'rous purple'll on and a dazzling cape!

Cupid says i'tu??!

she found out that this holiday was lost!

Daring C. wins!

No one says anything because we all know why Darling won!

Throw a Tea-rific *Tea Party*

Want to spellebrate in style with your Best Friends Forever After? Forget Princess Parties—they're so last chapter! Maddie Hatter knows that with a little preparation and some creative thinking, anyone can throw a tea party to remember! Try use her hat-tastic tips to create your own special event. Your guests are sure to be enchanted!

Cups and Kettles

You can't host a tea party without dishes, but don't risk the wrath of the Queen and borrow the family china. Scour thrift shops and rumble sales for mismatched, vintage plates and cups. The more patterned china on the table, the cuter it gets! Top everything off with the occasional statement piece, such as a tiered cake-stand.

Woodland Wonderland

You may not be able to transport your party to Wonderland, but that doesn't mean you can't set the scene. Set up several tables next to each other in your backyard, then string up garlands of fairy lights to create a touch of magic. If the weather's bad—don't panic. Fill vases, jelly jars and teapots with flowers to bring the outside in.

Clocks, Cats, Cards, and Chess

For a look that's really in keeping with Maddie's fabulous fable, place clocks around the table—just remember to set them all at "tea-time"! Hang up playing cards and add a cuddly "Cheshire" toy cat to a shelf or ledge. You also could put chess pieces around the party venue.

Inspiring Invites

When designing party invitations, take inspiration from *Alice's Adventures In Wonderland*. Shape each invite as a top hat or a tea cup. Don't forget to add a note to ask your guests to be punctual!

Dress Your Guests

Ask everyone to come dressed up as a character. They might choose to go all out as Alice or the Mad Hatter, or simply draw on some sweet mouse whiskers.

Eat Me/Drink Me

When it comes to food, think high tea. Serve sandwiches with the crusts cut off, iced buns or heart-shaped cookies. Make pink fizz by adding a squirt of lemon and a dash of cranberry juice to each glass of lemon-lime soda.

Fun and Frolics

Keep your guests amused with . . .

- A game of croquet.

- "Hunt the Queen". Take a pack of playing cards, then hide the Queen of Hearts somewhere for your guests to find.

- "Contrariwise". Give each guest a name sticker with their name written backwards—so for Alice write "ECILA". Guests must call each other by their contrariwise name or risk losing!

Magical Memories

For lasting memories, spray an old picture frame gold then take photographs of your guests "Through the Looking Glass" as they hold up the frame! Send them their picture as a thank you.

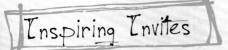

Latte Love

Royals and Rebels have a whole latte love for the foamy coffees from Hocus Latte in the village of Bookend. Do you love to sip drinks with your Best Friends Forever After? Try out this fabulous recipe for homemade gingerbread latte, then invite everyone over for a cup and a chat.

Ingredients:

For the syrup

- 16oz water
- 12oz granulated sugar
- 1 teaspoon ground cinnamon
- 2 teaspoons ground ginger
- ½ teaspoon vanilla extract

For the latte

- 4oz whole milk
- 1 tablespoon decaff instant coffee
- Can of whipped cream
- Ground cinnamon

Method:

1. First, make the gingerbread syrup. Mix the water and sugar with the cinnamon and ginger in a saucepan on the stove.

2. Bring the mixture to a boil, whisking as you go, then reduce the heat and simmer it for 15 minutes, stirring occasionally.

3. When the syrup has thickened, drop in the vanilla extract and allow it to cool.

You can store the syrup in an airtight bottle or tub in the fridge for two months. Always give it a shake before adding it to your latte.

4. To make a latte, pour the milk into a mug. Add the coffee and 3–4 tablespoons of your gingerbread syrup.

5. Stir everything together, then heat the mug in a microwave for 60 seconds.

6. Top the latte with a generous squirt of whipped cream. Sprinkle a dash of cinnamon, then sit back and enjoy . . . .

Always check in with an adult before making drinks that use boiling water.

Hopper's Epic Fairy Fails

Evelyne Spodluck
had a huge fairy
fail when she tryed to prank
a ~~teacher~~ ~~fae~~ teacher
by putting a jibberish spell
on the chairs in the teacher's
lounge.

Hopper Croakington II has a rather embarrassing habit of changing into a frog at exactly the wrong time. But Royal or Rebel, everyone has some funny fails in their story. Write some entries on the Mirror Blog telling everyone about your own hilarious trips and mishaps. Remember that time you slipped on a banana skin in the castleteria? Ever After High-ers want to read all about it!

CHAPTER THREE—*Magic and Mayhem*

True Hearts Day

As soon as newbie C.A. Cupid heard about True Hearts Day, she knew she had to put the holiday back on the Ever After High school calendar. It's all about embracing your true heart's desires!

Get into the mood by creating your own True Hearts collage. Collect mementoes of all the things or people that truly make you happy. You could use photos of friends, family, beloved pets, or hot crushes. Maybe you have ticket stubs, notes from your diary, or clippings from magazines? When you've gathered a pile of special souvenirs, stick them higgledy-piggledy into these frames. Whenever you look at them, your heart will leap with joy.

❧ Heart Art ❧

Photo frames are so last chapter. Make a heart-shaped photo collage for your wall! Choose your fairy, fairy best photos, then stick them in a heart formation using a low-tack adhesive. Spelltacular!

Raven Queen

Apple White

Madeline Hatter

Briar Beauty

Magical Crafts

Cedar Wood **is** hextremely artistic. Can you help the wooden one with her latest art homework a**ss**ignment?

Cedar's Sculpture

Cedar has been asked to sketch a design for a sculpture with the title "And they lived Happily Ever After...". It should be a fun project, but she's suffering from artist's block! Can you help her?

Ashlynn's Princess-and-the-Pea Bed

Ashlynn has created a cute miniature bed for her Princessology class. Would you like to make one, too? It would look enchanting on any shelf or bedside table.

You will need:

- A large empty matchbox
- Wooden craft sticks
- Craft and fabric glue
- Adhesive tape
- Green bead or dried pea
- Coffee stirrers or toothpicks
- Pretty scraps of material
- Scissors
- Needle and thread
- Cotton balls

What you do:

1. Open the large matchbox and discard the sleeve. If you want to make a really sturdy bed, you could also glue craft sticks to the inside.

2. Create four tall bedposts by gluing two craft sticks together end-to-end for each post.

3. Glue each post to a corner of the matchbox using tape to hold the pieces in place while the glue dries. If you need to, glue horizontal struts half way up between the bedposts (at the seam of the craft sticks) to make the structure more stable.

4. Now stick a "pea" to the base of the matchbox—you could use a green bead or a dried pea.

5. Create a ladder using more crafts sticks, coffee stirrers, or toothpicks.

6. Next, pick your fabric scraps—you'll need around 15. Cut them so that when folded in half, they fit the size of the matchbox.

7. Turn each fabric scrap inside out, fold it in half, and then sew or glue up the two sides.

You should now have a sort of mini envelope. Repeat with all the scraps.

8. Next turn all of the scraps the right way out and stuff them with a small amount of cotton balls so that they become squishy. Sew or glue the last edges closed.

9. Choose a smaller square scrap of material for the pillow, then stitch and stuff as before.

10. Pile the mattresses up on the bed and enjoy your mini masterpiece!

Always stay scissor safe!

49

The Tale of Legacy Day

I t's Legacy Day at Ever After High—the day the students pledge to follow their predestined paths through life. Raven Queen, however, has other ideas . . . .

Legacy Day dawned at Ever After High.

Students pledge to follow the path of their fairy-tale parents . . . .

Maddie, you have to help me!

. . . or not!

Raven had cold feet.

Maddie Hatter didn't exactly put Raven's mind at rest.

Meanwhile Apple White and Blondie Lockes were talking in the hall . . .

I don't feel like I wanna sign the *Storybook of Legends.* But I don't want to let anyone down.

Don't forget the whole you-may-vanish-into-oblivion thing.

See, I am totally a Royal!

. . . Raven whisked Maddie away.

. . . when . . .

Raven! There you are. We have to talk.

Raven— come back!

I have to convince Raven to sign the book. My destiny depends on it.

Maddie took Raven to the Vault of Lost Tales.

She knocked and they were magically spirited inside.

Apple arrived just a second too late.

Raven?

The girls had vanished.

If anyone knows the truth about the *Storybook of Legends*, it's Giles Grimm.

The headmaster's brother welcomed them with open arms . . . .

Raven had no idea what he was saying.

He was cursed with a Babble Spell. Makes him sound cuckoo!

Feathers and friends, together alone!

Luckily Maddie could understand Riddlish.

He says it's nice to have us here.

Ask him about the book. If I don't sign, am I really gonna disappear?

. . . and Giles Grimm answered.

Maddie translated.

So, Maddie asked . . .

The King who sings with pages of sky fears too much the dawn that rises with lies.

He says there's something wrong with the book and if you don't sign . . . .

What?

Raven waited in horror for the final part of Giles's message . . .

P.T.O.

Eventually Maddie finished her sentence.

If you don't sign, your story will continue . . . I think.

That evening . . . .

. . . but Maddie and Giles had begun to have tea.

You think!?

Riddlish is not an exact language!

Next we have Apple White.

I am Apple White, daughter of Snow White.

A key appeared out of thin air and floated to Apple's hand. It was time to open the *Storybook of Legends*.

Apple came onto the stage to great applause.

Apple saw her destiny laid out in its pages.

Apple's friends went wild.

In the mirror she saw herself as queen.

And in the flutter of a fairy's wing she signed the book.

Apple White

52

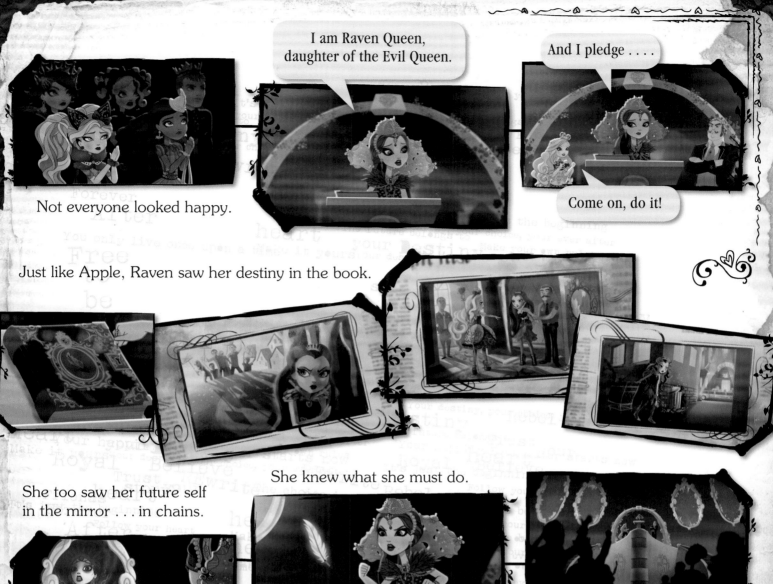

Not everyone looked happy.

I am Raven Queen, daughter of the Evil Queen.

And I pledge . . . .

Come on, do it!

Just like Apple, Raven saw her destiny in the book.

She knew what she must do.

She too saw her future self in the mirror . . . in chains.

I'm going to write my own destiny—my Happily Ever After starts now!

Raven shut the book without signing. The mirrors smashed.

Raven and her friends were ecstatic.

Raven had stood up for what she believed . . . .

The great Royal/Rebel divide began.

I'm still here! I didn't disappear!

I'm sorry but I don't want anyone to tell me who to be. I'm not the only one who gets to choose a new destiny—we all do!

You're still here, yay!

It feels good!

Whether she'd honored her destiny or tempted fate—she still had Best Friends Forever After.

But Apple was devastated.

I don't want a new destiny.

THE END

Briar's Study Party

It was a sunny day at Ever After High . . .

You heard correctly Raven Queen!

. . . but things weren't so sunny in Professor Rumpelstiltskin's classroom.

Um, Professor, this is totally unfair.

You can't test us on chapters one to thirty-four.

We've studied only up to chapter two!

The students were up in arms . . .

Cedar Wood chimed in . . . .

Mwah ha ha!

That night the students met in the Throne Room to discuss the situation.

The Professor seemed to be enjoying the injustice.

I cannot tell a lie and that's just not very nice!

Blondie Lockes filled everyone in . . . .

Then Briar piped in.

I could tutor you guys. I've been studying on my own forever after.

At the beginning of every year he gives an insanely hard test so students have to ask for extra credit.

The test is tomorrow— I'm getting stress splinters!

Royally cool.

It sounded like a great plan.

Zzzzzz . . . .

The friends desperately tried to wake Briar.

Let's start with . . . yawn!

Daring tried dazzling her awake with his smile.

Nothing!

The boys snapped books shut next to her ears.

Blondie even sent a terrifying bear hologram via her Mirror Pad.

Briar Beauty did not stir.

P.T.O.

All seemed lost until . . .

If only she took studying as seriously as she does partying!

That's it!

. . . Dexter gave Raven an idea.

Hey guys, what's up?

You are up . . . finally! Now you have to stay awake and help us.

There's one thing I'm always up for!

After just a few beats of party music, the sleeping beauty awoke.

A study party!

The basic elements.

Briar began tutoring her friends.

They worked all night . . .

There's pixie dust and dragon fire.

56

Pixie dust and dragon fire!

All too soon it was morning and time for the test.

. . . repeating the lessons to music, while dancing around the Throne Room.

Time's up. Let's see how you've failed!

The professor cast a spell to gather in the test papers.

He began to magically grade them.

Professor Rumpelstiltskin got redder and redder.

Raven Queen . . . an A!

Apple White . . . an A!

Cedar Wood . . . A? Hunter Huntsman . . . A! Aaaaaargh!

The As went on and on . . . . . . and on!

Never underestimate the power of a study party!

Roooarrrrgh!

The students had done it!

The End

CHAPTER FOUR—*Sorcery and Stories*

The *Shoe* Must Go On

Use your enchanting drawing skills to complete the story where you see this quill.

Ashlynn was waiting for a very special delivery.

Suddenly the door opened.

> I hope that's you, Hunter.

> I got shoes! Now how about a hug for your hero.

> Thank you so much for getting these!

But then Ashlynn made her guy leave.

It was!

> Briar and Blondie are going to be here any minute, and they can't know about us.

Just then Briar and Blondie arrived at the store. Ashlynn thanked them for coming to help.

Blondie immediately got bossy . . .

> No problem, Ashlynn. I see where you have the platforms. I'll move them so the natural light gives them that halo effect.

. . . and the clock was ticking.

Meanwhile outside, Hunter was being pelted with nuts by Pesky—his squirrel nemesis.

Hordes of shoppers started to arrive.

The door flew open. Hunter and Pesky burst in.

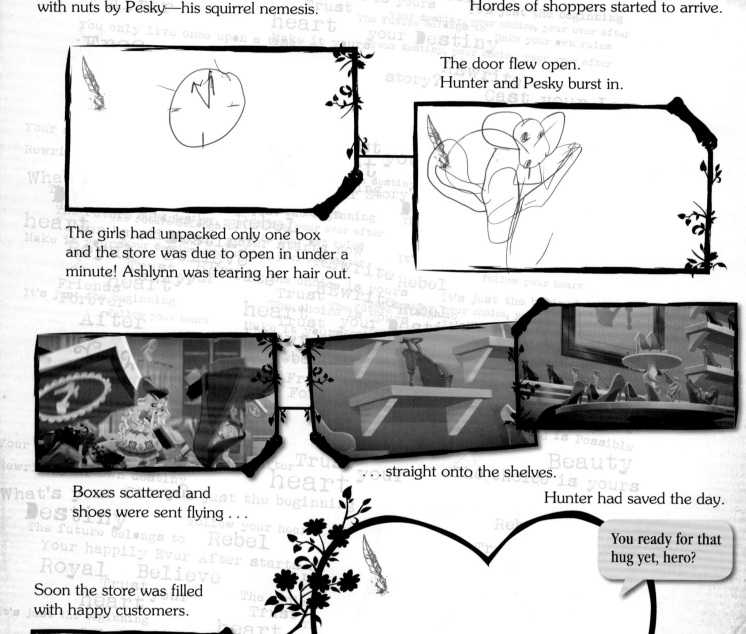

The girls had unpacked only one box and the store was due to open in under a minute! Ashlynn was tearing her hair out.

. . . straight onto the shelves.

Boxes scattered and shoes were sent flying . . .

Hunter had saved the day.

You ready for that hug yet, hero?

Soon the store was filled with happy customers.

Wow, do we get free shoes for helping, or what?

THE END

You Shall Go To The Ball . . .

Start Here

... or dance or **sleepover**! Briar Beauty loves to party. She spends all her free time on the Royal Student Council planning the next big social gathering. What kind of get-together gets you going? Take this fun quiz to find out. Just pick your preferences and follow the arrows.

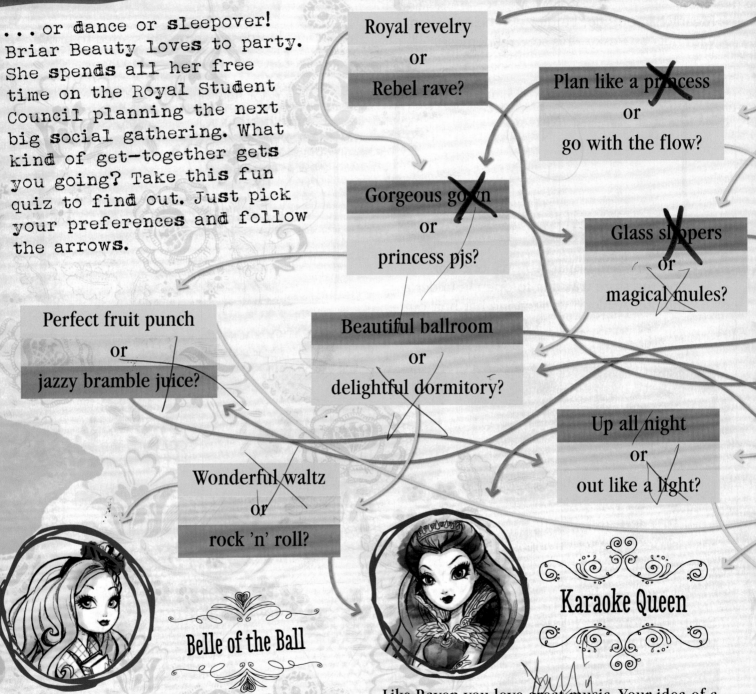

Royal revelry
or
Rebel rave?

Plan like a princess
or
go with the flow?

Gorgeous gown
or
princess pjs?

Glass slippers
or
magical mules?

Perfect fruit punch
or
jazzy bramble juice?

Beautiful ballroom
or
delightful dormitory?

Up all night
or
out like a light?

Wonderful waltz
or
rock 'n' roll?

Belle of the Ball

Mirror, Mirror, on the wall, don't you just adore a ball? Fairy-tale Fourteenth or Thronecoming bash, you love everything from the first preparations to the big entrance. You and Apple were both born for grand occasions!

Karaoke Queen

Like Raven you love great music. Your idea of a party is a chance to sing your heart out. You don't care what others think of your outfit, and you don't need a prince on your arm. You just want to have fun and see where the night takes you!

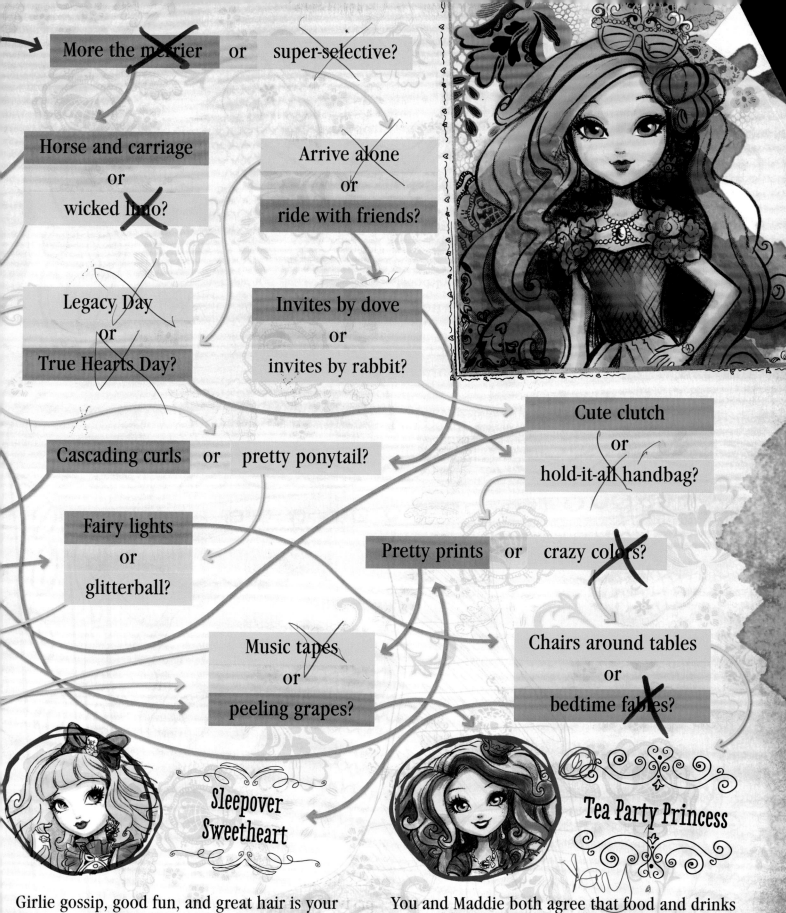

More the merrier ~~or~~ super-selective?

Horse and carriage or ~~wicked limo?~~

Arrive alone or ride with friends?

Legacy Day or True Hearts Day?

Invites by dove or invites by rabbit?

Cute clutch or hold-it-all handbag?

Cascading curls or pretty ponytail?

Fairy lights or glitterball?

Pretty prints or crazy colors?

Music tapes or peeling grapes?

Chairs around tables or bedtime fables?

Sleepover Sweetheart

Tea Party Princess

Girlie gossip, good fun, and great hair is your idea of the perfect get-together. Just like Blondie, you're never happier than when you're in your pajamas practicing party-ready hairdos on your Best Friends Forever After.

You and Maddie both agree that food and drinks are the key to any wonderful event. You love hosting a party with tasty treats and tea. Friends flock to your brilliant brunches, lovely lunches, and happy high teas.

Slippery Scenario

Ashlynn Ella can't resist fancy footwear, but she's so over glass slippers. Grab your quill and ink, then design and sketch the perfect party shoe.

Glamsel in Distress

When Briar Beauty was on her way to the Spring Fairest Ball, disaster struck. The unfortunate Royal snagged her gown on a prickly thorn bush. Luckily, in Princessology class, students learn to think on their dainty-toed feet! Briar's enchantingly innovative twists transformed a buttoned shirt into a fairy unique look. Would you like to make one of your own?

Try some shirt couture! One piece can be worn in so many ways!
All you need is an oversized handsome prince's shirt (your elder brother's or father's will do) with long sleeves.

The Bow Belle

1. Open the buttons on the shirt and tuck the collar inside.

2. Wrap the shirt around yourself like a towel, with the buttons in front.

3. Adjust the shirt so it's comfortable, then fasten a button at chest level—fourth button down should give you a sweetheart neckline, while the second or third will give a straighter shape.

4. Take the sleeves and tie them in front in a bow. If you're really clever, you could even ball them up to create a rose.

The Bombspell

1. Keep the collar of the shirt turned out rather than tucked in.

2. Wrap the shirt around your body, but wear it backwards so that the buttons fasten at the back.

3. Wrap the sleeves behind you and tie them up to create a bow.

4. Now add a thin belt in a contrasting color to crown your cute new outfit.

Fairy Tale Hair

Rapunzel's Tower Hair Salon is the place to go for head-turning tresses. Here are three of the salon's signature looks for this season. Most valued customer Blondie Lockes gives her verdict on each style, while Holly O'Hair shares her tips for fabulous fairy-tale hair!

1. Dampen your hair and comb it through, then gather the strands into a ponytail at the top of your head.

2. Secure the hair with an elastic—if you would normally make two loops with the elastic, then pull the ponytail through once completely but stop halfway the second time round, so that your hair is in a loop at the top of your head with the ends hanging out.

3. Take the knot of hair and pull it into two sections— to make the two sides of the bow.

4. Grab the elastic, twist and put over one of the sections. You should now be left with a bun in two loops.

5. Take the tail end of your ponytail and wrap it over the space between the two loops of the bun.

6. Tuck the ends below the bun and secure them with hair grips.

7. Adjust the bow by tweaking the size of the loops.

8. Pin any stray ends, and spritz with hairspray.

The Bow Bun

(for very long hair)

Hair tools

- A wide-tooth comb
- Hair elastics
- Cute hair slides or clips
- Hair grips
- Hairspray

Verdict: Take a bow! A fairy fabulous hairdo for the belle of the ball.

The Double Twist

(for short to mid-length hair)

1. Use a wide-tooth comb to remove tangles from your hair.
2. Part the hair in the center or slightly to one side.
3. Gather a 1-inch section of hair from the right side of the head.
4. Tightly twist the hair clockwise (toward the parting rather than away from it).
5. Keeping the twist close to the scalp, work in more strands of hair as you move toward the crown.
6. Secure the twist with a pretty clip, before doing the same on the other side.

 Verdict: *Gorgeous, girlie, and glam!*

The Inverse Ponytail

(for mid to long-length hair)

1. Pull your hair back into a low ponytail and secure it with an elastic.
2. Now use your fingers to make a hole in your hair just above the band.
3. Take the end of the ponytail and pull it up, over and down through the hole to create a cute, twisted look.
4. Tighten up the look by splitting the ponytail in two and pulling down on it.
5. Spritz the style with hairspray to hold it in place.
6. As an extra finishing touch, add some cute jewels or flower-headed pins to the twist.

 Verdict: *Quick, queenly, and stunning!*

Holly's Hexcellent Hair Tips

Don't wash your hair every day; this will dry it out and weigh it down. For most people, three to four times a week is plenty.

Use a conditioner on the ends of your hair to add shine—homemade treatments can be just as good. Try mixing equal parts of mayonnaise with puréed avocado.

Hair is most fragile when it's wet. Never rough towel-dry it or brush it after a wash. Instead blot your hair with a towel to remove excess moisture, then use a wide-tooth comb to remove tangles, working from the ends up, not from the roots down.

Mirror, Mirror, . . .

. . . in the bin, let's give you a cool new spin! Where would a princess or, in fact, any girl be without a mirror? Now you can make your own custom looking glass and do your part for the environment. Each Ever After High pupil has chosen her favorite way to upcycle an old, flat-framed mirror. Which one will you choose?

Always ask an adult before starting a new craft project! Be careful with knives and scissors.

Maddie's Wonderlandiful Looking Glass

You will need:
- Old costume jewelery, brooches, and pendants
- Buttons, bottle tops, badges, seashells
- Craft glue
- Flat-framed mirror

What to do:
1. Start a collection of colorful buttons, old costume jewelery and anything else that catches your eye. You could scour rummage sales and thrift shops or pick up objects when you go out for a walk.

2. Starting with a small section, apply some glue to the frame. Cover the sticky patch with jewels and buttons. Move onto the next section of the frame.

3. Work your way around the mirror until the whole frame is a riot of color. Leave it to dry fully.

Raven's Musical Mirror

You will need:
- Old CDs
- Scissors
- Craft glue
- Flat-framed mirror

What to do:
1. Ask an adult to help you cut the CDs into pieces.

2. Apply a little glue to a small area on the frame, then gently fix pieces of CD onto it. Stick the shapes play-side up.

3. Continue on sticking until the whole frame is covered with a mosaic of CD shards. Leave the mirror to dry before hanging it on the wall.

Ashlynn's Wild Woodland Mirror

You will need:

- A selection of twigs of approximately the same length. All should be roughly 1 inch in diameter.
- Wood glue
- Flat-framed mirror

What to do:

1. Make sure the twigs are completely dry and moss-free.

2. Start gluing the twigs to the frame. You could do this so that they lie neatly side-by-side with one end pointing to the mirror and the other out. Otherwise try creating a wilder more tangled look by bunching the twigs up and laying them around the frame.

3. When the mirror is fully dry, put it on display.

Briar's Party Popper Mirror

You will need:

- Used party popper containers
- Craft glue
- Flat-framed mirror

What to do:

1. Check that all of the poppers have been fired off already.

2. Apply glue to an area of the mirror and stick the poppers on—this looks most effective if you alternate the colors of the poppers and the direction they face.

3. Continue until the frame is covered. For an extra touch, you could stick some streamers in among the party poppers.

EPILOGUE

Answers

Pages 28-29

Quiz for a Queen

1. b
2. a
3. They all come from Wonderland
4. It is bottomless and full of items for every occasion.
5. Ashlynn Ella, daughter of Cinderella
6. Cerise Hood. Her parents Red Riding Hood and the Big Bad Wolf ended up getting married.
7. c
8. Pinocchio
9. c
10. C.A. Cupid. She transferred from Monster High.
11. Riddlish
12. b
13. Daring and Dexter Charming
14. Snow White and the Seven Dwarves (Apple White) and Little Red Riding Hood (Cerise Hood)
15. The Frog Prince

Page 30

Sports Day: Dragon Slaying

POSITION	NAME	NUMBER	COLOR
First Place	Daring	4	Red
Second Place	Sparrow	2	Green
Third Place	Dexter	1	Blue
Fourth Place	Hunter	3	Yellow

Sports Day: Basketball

21

Page 31

Wicked "Where" Wordsearch?

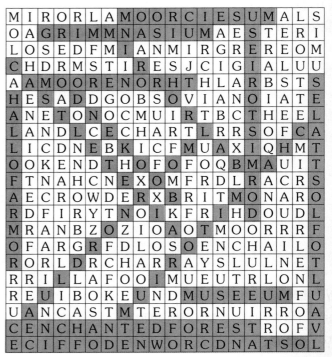

Page 34

Witch Prof?

A) Coach Gingerbreadman
B) Professor Momma Bear
C) Professor Poppa Bear
D) Mr. Jack. B. Nimble
E) Professor Rumpelstiltskin
F) Professor Pied Piper

Coming Soon to EVER AFTER HIGH:

The *Spring Unsprung* Fair 2015

It's going to be totally hexcellent!